Tusks

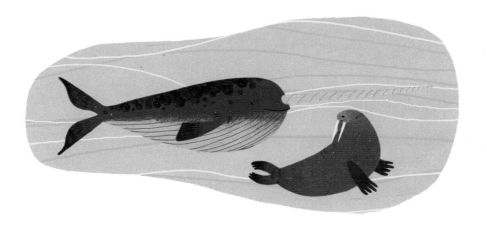

Written by Jane Clarke

Illustrated by Jean Claude

Collins

Winston had sleek tusks.
But Norman had just one tusk.
It had twists and a sharp point.

Winston and Norman went hunting for food.

Norman swam at high speed.
But he did not fish well.

Winston's tusks were scooping
lots of clams. He kept boasting,
"My tusks are better than yours!"

They did not see the storm creep up on them. All of a sudden, the wind was howling.

There was hail and sleet. The storm was majestic – and frightening! Norman was screeching, "Look out!"

They had to flee at speed from
the storm.

Crash!

Winston's tusks were stuck. He was groaning, "Norman, I need your help! My tusks cannot free me."

Norman was smart. His tusk was
spearing and twisting to free Winston.

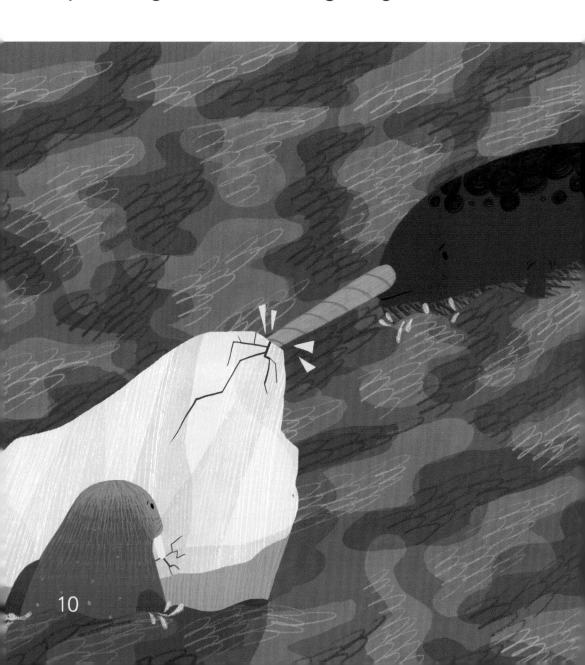

Then there was a crack.
Norman's tusk set Winston free!

Three tusks were sparkling in the starlight.

Norman said, "Winston, your tusks are best for you, but one long tusk is best for me."

Winston agreed. "We love our tusks!"

Three tusks

:paw: **After reading** :paw:

Letters and Sounds: Phase 4

Word count: 164

Focus on adjacent consonants with long vowel phonemes, e.g. /s/ /p/ /ee/ /d/

Common exception words: of, to, the, all, are, my, he, me, was, you, they, said, were, there, one, out, your, love, our

Curriculum links: Science: Animals

National Curriculum learning objectives: Spoken language: articulate and justify answers, arguments and opinions; Reading/Word reading: apply phonic knowledge and skills as the route to decoding words, read accurately by blending sounds in unfamiliar words containing GPCs that have been taught, read other words of more than one syllable that contain taught GPCs, read aloud accurately books that are consistent with their developing phonic knowledge; Reading/Comprehension: understand both the books they can already read accurately ... by: making inferences on the basis of what is being said and done

Developing fluency

- Your child may enjoy hearing you read the story.
- You could read the book together, with you reading the main text on each page and your child reading the dialogue. Encourage them to read with expression, particularly in the storm scene.

Phonic practice

- Support your child to practise reading words with adjacent consonants and long vowel sounds. You may wish to model carrying out the following task before you ask your child to do the same.
- Ask your child to:
  - o Use your finger to draw a line under each sound.
  - o Now read each sound and then blend the word.

b/oa/s/t	boast	s/c/r/ee/ch	screech
g/r/oa/n	groan	s/p/ea/r/ing	spearing
f/r/igh/t/e/n/i/n/g	frightening		

Extending vocabulary

- Read page 7 to your child. Can they think of other words to describe the storm? (e.g. *scary, powerful*)